Sharing Bear Hugs

Encouraging children to develop a love
of books helps their literacy now and makes a difference
to their whole future.

One of the main ways you can do this is by reading
aloud. It's never too early to start – even small babies enjoy
being read to – and it's important to carry on, even when
children can read for themselves.

Choose a time that suits you both and a place
that's comfortable.

Don't worry about being good at reading.
A parent's voice is one of the sounds that children love best.
Encourage them to join in with rhymes or repeated phrases,
and to tell you the story in their own words.

Take time to look at the pictures together.
Pictures help tell the story that's written, but often
tell their own stories too.

It's a good sign if children comment and ask questions as
you read. It shows they're interested. Talk about the book.
Was it good? Were there any favourite moments?

Read aloud as often as you can – new stories
and old favourites!

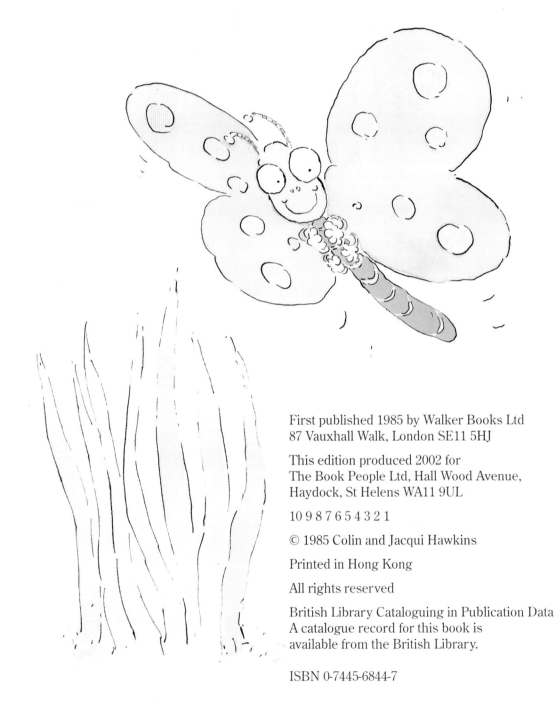

First published 1985 by Walker Books Ltd
87 Vauxhall Walk, London SE11 5HJ

This edition produced 2002 for
The Book People Ltd, Hall Wood Avenue,
Haydock, St Helens WA11 9UL

10 9 8 7 6 5 4 3 2 1

© 1985 Colin and Jacqui Hawkins

Printed in Hong Kong

British Library Cataloguing in Publication Data
A catalogue record for this book is
available from the British Library.

ISBN 0-7445-6844-7

Where's My Mummy?

Colin and Jacqui Hawkins

TED SMART

Bear Hugs is a range of bright and lively picture books by some of today's very best authors and illustrators. Each book contains a page of friendly notes on reading and is perfect for parents and children to share.

Cuddle up with a Bear Hug today!